A Message for
GENERAL
WASHINGTON

by Vivian Schurfranz

SILVER MOON PRESS
NEW YORK

First Silver Moon Press Edition 1998

Copyright © 1998 by Vivian Schurfranz
Project Editor: Wendy Wax
Cover Illustration: John F. Martin
Historical Fact Checking:
Kevin P. Kelly, Colonial Williamsburg Foundation;
John Short, Colonial National Historic Park

For information:
Silver Moon Press
New York, NY
(800) 874-3320

Library of Congress Cataloging-in-Publication Data

Schurfranz, Vivian.
A Message for General Washington/by Vivian Schurfranz
p. cm. -- (Stories of the States)
Summary: Twelve-year-old Hannah accepts the challenge of sneak-
ing behind enemy lines to deliver a message to General Washington,
which will result in the British surrender at Yorktown.
ISBN 1-881889-89-0
1. Yorktown (Va.)--History--Siege, 1781--Juvenile fiction.
[1. Yorktown (Va.)--History--Siege, 1781--Fiction. 2. Virginia--
History--Revolution, 1775-1783--Fiction. 3. United States--History--
Revolution, 1775-1783--Fiction.] I. Title. II. Series.
PZ7.S397Me 1998
[Fic]--dc21
98-15800
CIP
AC
10 9 8 7 6 5 4 3 2 1

Printed in the USA

★★★ TABLE OF CONTENTS ≡

STORIES OF THE STATES

CHAPTER ONE
Hannah Confronts a Redcoat

HANNAH WINSLOW FELT PRETTY AND grown-up as she hurried to the waterfront. It was not every day that her mother allowed her to wear her next-to-best green gingham dress. But it wasn't every day she went to the river either. Since early August, her mother had been warning her to stay close to home, for there were eight thousand British soldiers occupying Yorktown. But Hannah refused to feel threatened. This was *her* town, and she wasn't going to let the British troops take it over for their own! Sometimes it seemed that her mother forgot she was twelve years old. Why, she still protected her like a mother cat protects her kittens!

As Hannah untied the yellow ribbon in her hair, the few copper coins in her dress pocket—enough money to buy oysters for dinner—clinked together. She shook her head, freeing her long auburn curls. A warm breeze blew lightly against her skin. What could happen to her on such a sunny day in early September?

"Hey, rebel girl!" came a harsh, crackling voice.

Glancing sideways, Hannah noticed a Redcoat emerging from the Swan Tavern across the street. She ignored her quickening pulse and kept walking.

"Stop, rebel! I'm talking to *you!*"

As the Redcoat moved toward her, Hannah halted and turned. "What do you want?" she demanded, staring at him with her cold green eyes. His red, puffy face and red knee-length crimson coat, which was cut up the back like two tails, made him resemble a lobster. *A boiled lobster!* Hannah thought, smothering a smile.

"Come here!" the Redcoat roared, as he came closer. He was holding out a pair of boots. "Take these to the cobbler for a polish!"

"I'm on an errand for my mother," Hannah said crisply, feeling the anger rise up inside her. She wanted to say, *Carry your own boots!* But her heart was beating too fast.

The Redcoat's face grew redder and puffier. "You're supposed to serve your masters!" he yelled, throwing the boots at her feet. "Pick them up and be on your way, you rebel snippet! I'll collect them in an hour."

"I can't!" Hannah said, glaring at him, her fists on her hips. She tried to appear brave, though inside, a wave of fear washed over her.

"What do you mean you *can't?*" The Redcoat thundered. "You Colonials need to be taught a lesson! Always so high and mighty—even when you're losing the war!" He stepped even closer and squinted down at her. "I'm about to teach you who your masters are!" He lifted his hand as if to strike—but then hesitated. "Be gone," he muttered, grabbing his boots and walking away.

Greatly relieved, and still a bit shaky, Hannah tossed her hair over her shoulders and continued toward Ballard Street. Oh, how she hated these British! But at least she'd held her ground. If only her father, who was away in General Washington's army, would come swooping down and drive General Cornwallis and his Redcoats into Chesapeake Bay! Hannah sighed. She missed her father—a tall dark-haired man with a warm, friendly grin. He'd been away for three long years. She hoped he was in good health and would soon return home. She wondered if he missed making furniture. He made the finest cabinets in town.

Hannah turned down Ballard Street and descended to the lower town—what once had been a busy, noisy port. Now the only vessels on the river were British war ships. She walked past fish stands with Chesapeake crabs and mackerel set out in rows.

"Over here!" shouted an old fisherman. "I trapped these crabs this morning!"

Hannah shook her head and headed over to a fisherman's oyster stand. She bought a pint of oysters with the few coppers her mother had managed to save. Then, instead of wandering around as she usually did, she headed straight home. She was so eager to tell her mother what had happened, she practically ran through the streets. If her mother could see her now, she'd say, A young lady must walk slowly, hold her shoulders back, and look straight ahead. But Hannah didn't care. Not today.

She rushed past the white church with its tall steeple, the block of mansions, and the blacksmith shop. She glanced briefly at Secretary Thomas Nelson's brick house with its serene gardens and sundial. One would never guess that General Cornwallis, the British commander, used it as his headquarters. During the war the Redcoats had taken over many houses, causing the residents to flee.

"Where are you going so fast, Hannah?" said a familiar voice.

Startled, Hannah looked up and saw Martin Jamison, the blacksmith, standing outside his shop. "I can't stop to talk," she said to the strong, wide-shouldered man.

"Run along then," said Martin. "I'll be over to see you later. I have some news."

Picking up her stride, Hannah wondered what Martin's news was. Being something of a spy—and the unofficial courier of Yorktown—Martin always had news. Though he had requested to join the Continental Army, he'd been asked to stay in Yorktown, where his blacksmithing and other skills were needed.

Hannah didn't slow down until she reached her front gate. Then panting, she walked around the house to the kitchen. The tantalizing aroma of stew, which simmered over the fireplace coals, filled the air.

"Mother!" Hannah called, unable to hide the excitement in her voice. When no one answered, she went out to the backyard. There she saw her mother churning butter. Her light-colored hair hung in wisps about her heart-shaped face as she turned the paddle in quick circular motions.

"Mother, I was stopped by a British soldier," said Hannah.

Her mother looked worried. "Why did he stop you, Hannah? What were you doing?"

Why did her mother always think it was *her* fault? "I was just minding my own business, and this Redcoat ordered me to take his boots to the cobbler," said Hannah.

"And did you?" her mother asked, wiping her hands on her long apron. She took the oysters from Hannah and gently dropped them in the stew.

"I wouldn't touch his old boots!" Hannah said, indignantly. "But I didn't sass him either." She didn't mention how scared she'd been.

Mrs. Winslow shook her head, her pale complexion glistening with perspiration. "Hannah, I wish you wouldn't be so daring. He could have struck you."

"He almost did," Hannah said, proud that she had been so brave. "But then he thought better of it."

"Sometimes I think you invite trouble, Hannah," Mrs. Winslow said, beginning to churn more fiercely. "I often wish you could be more like your older sister, Pegg."

Not caring to hear another word, Hannah stomped away. Why did her mother have to compare her to Pegg all the time? It seemed as if her older sister always did the right thing, and Hannah always did the wrong thing. Pegg was a lot more like their mother—soft-spoken, sweet, and mannerly. Even though Pegg had moved to Williamsburg with her new husband, David, their mother still compared the two of them. *I guess I'll always live in Pegg's perfect shadow,* Hannah thought miserably. However, in some ways, it really wasn't so bad. She didn't care to be perfect and never have any fun. She liked herself just the way she was. If only her mother could like her that way, too!

There was a knock on the front door. When Hannah opened it to find Martin, she invited him in. Hannah liked Martin; his presence in the town gave her a sense of security, especially with her father, and so many other men, away.

"Where's your mother?" Martin asked.

"She's out back," Hannah said.

Martin opened the back door and yelled, "Maude! Come inside!"

Moments later the three of them were seated around a table in the main room. "I have some good news," said Martin. "Admiral de Grasse and his navy were spotted on the Chesapeake last week."

"That's wonderful!" said Hannah. "Now the French navy will guard the bay to prevent the Redcoats from getting any reinforcements."

"We mustn't get our hopes up," said Mrs. Winslow.

Hannah sighed. Why did her mother have to be so pessimistic?

"We have a good chance, though," said Martin.

He reached into his vest pocket and pulled out a tattered envelope.

"A letter!" Hannah shouted. "Is it from Father?"

"It sure is!" Martin's broad face beamed as he handed

the letter to Hannah's mother.

"You read it, Martin," Mrs. Winslow begged, clutching her hands together in her lap.

Ever since the war had begun, Martin had been helping to smuggle mail between soldiers and their families. In doing this, he often got secret reports regarding movements of British troops. He cleared his throat and began to read:

September 3, 1781
Near Chester, Pennsylvania

Dear Maude and Hannah,

I'm writing this by candlelight as there's no time to write during the day. General George Washington's regiment had a long march beginning in New York. We crossed the Hudson River at King's Ferry, and now we're moving south. We've walked for months. How I wish I had enlisted in the cavalry! We just passed through Philadelphia, and we hope to arrive at head of Elk by week's end. It is rumored that Washington will visit his wife at Mt. Vernon. I don't blame him. It's been six years since he's seen his home. Our troops should reach Williamsburg soon. There, I hope to receive a twenty-four-hour leave to see Pegg.

All is well in the Continental camp, but we've been away from our families for much too long. It seems like ages since

Lexington and Concord—the beginning of everything. The Americans are tired and worn down after all these years. Our uniforms are tattered and we ache to go home. I must say, though, that General Washington keeps our spirits up. Once again we're ready and eager for battle. And this time we'll win.

Maude, my dear wife, I hope you're well and holding down the home front. And, Hannah, mind what your mother says. Please remember that I love each of you and you're constantly in my thoughts. I'll soon be home—I promise. Ah, to be back in my woodworking shop! Maude, I plan to make you a beautiful mahogany chair if you'll let me take a rest in it. It will seem like heaven after what I've been through!

With deep affection,
Father

When Martin handed the letter to Maude, she broke the silence with a sigh. Hannah yearned to comfort her mother. She wanted to squeeze her hand, but was afraid her mother would pull away and caution her to be brave. She wiped away a tear of her own. It was hard to be brave when her father was away and in danger. If only he'd return. Then they'd be a family again. Sometimes, though, Hannah felt that day would never come.

CHAPTER TWO
Sad News

"WE NEED A HOT FIRE FOR CANDLE-making," Mrs. Winslow said to Hannah later that afternoon. With that, Hannah threw another log on the fire. Then she reached for one of the candle rods her mother had brought in, and twisted several wicks of entwined hemp. When she was finished, she dipped the hemp into the tallow, and then hung it on the rod to cool. Later, when it was cool and hard, she would dip it again to make the candle thicker.

Although Hannah enjoyed making candles, working over the blazing fire could be very uncomfortable. So when her mother suggested that Hannah go out to play while she finished up, Hannah was relieved.

"Mother, may I go over to Elizabeth's house to see if she can go down to the river?" Hannah remembered to call Lizzie "Elizabeth" in front of her mother.

"I suppose so," Mrs. Winslow answered. "But be careful and mind you're not late for dinner. I'm having your favorite—fish stew and hot biscuits."

"Sounds delicious," Hannah said, unconvincingly. "I won't be late, I promise."

Happily, Hannah hurried to Lizzie Reston's house. The Restons lived three houses away in an impressive two-story, Georgian-style home. The two houses in between were empty, their neighbors having fled Yorktown like many other families. As the British troops turned Yorktown into a garrison village, many found that life there had become intolerable. Some fled to the Piedmonts and the Valley of Virginia after the war began. Others joined relatives in Fredericksburg or Petersburg. Some people feared for their own lives because they were identified as Patriots. But the Restons and the Winslows refused to leave.

Just as Hannah was about to knock, Lizzie opened the door.

"I saw you coming," said Lizzie, smiling warmly. The two girls hugged.

Hannah admired her best friend. Her blond hair was neatly plaited, and her blue eyes and long lashes made her the prettiest girl in Yorktown. At least Hannah thought so. Today she wore a blue frilled gown. "Mother said I have to dress nicely for dinner," said Lizzie. "The Langtrys are invited over."

"Can you come to the river with me?" Hannah asked hopefully.

"My mother won't let me," said Lizzie.

"Don't tell her," Hannah pleaded.

"I can't be gone more than an hour," said Lizzie.

"Me neither," said Hannah. "I have to be back for dinner, too."

"Then let's go." Lizzie skipped down the front steps, her lacy skirts flouncing.

Yorktown, one of the most beautiful towns of the southern colonies, sat high above the York River. Hannah often realized how lucky she was to live in such a scenic place. Even the presence of the British troops could not take away its pristine beauty.

"I'm getting tired of seafood," said Hannah as they took the steep Great Valley path to the river. That was all anyone ate these days—except for the British troops, who frequently foraged for cattle from nearby plantations.

"Me too," said Lizzie, wrinkling her nose. "Bessie, our cook, is trying a *new* seafood dish—swordfish patties. Mother is worried to death that the Langtrys might not like it."

They glimpsed the river—sparkling blue in the

afternoon sunlight—as they reached the bottom of the path. Hannah hurriedly took off her shoes and stockings and with a *whoop*, ran into the river. Lizzie followed. They splashed into the warm water, careful not to wet their hair.

As they stood in the waist-deep water, Hannah wiggled her toes in the squishy mud. "Come on, Lizzie," she urged, taking her friend's hand. "Let's wade upriver."

The girls waded upriver and then downriver, talking about everything as they always did. Finally, exhausted, they climbed onto a sand bar to dry off. Lizzie removed her white lace cap.

"I like how you plaited your hair," Hannah said, admiring Lizzie's sleek and shiny, thick braid.

"You don't know how lucky you are, Hannah," said Lizzie. "You can just brush your hair and let it fly." She reached over, fingering an auburn curl that fell across Hannah's shoulder. "It looks so natural. I have to work and work to force my hair into a plait."

"We're both lucky." Hannah laughed, touching Lizzie's hand. "You with your blond tresses and me with my auburn ones."

Then Hannah remembered something. "I almost forgot to tell you. We had a letter from Father today."

"You did?" Lizzie's face lit up. "Where is he? What

did he say?"

"He's still with General Washington. He should be in Williamsburg soon." Hannah's face grew serious. "But Lizzie, he misses us. I think as much as we miss him!"

"We miss your father, too," said Lizzie, smiling. "Mother can't wait for his return so he can make a table for the dining room."

"Well, it won't be long till both our fathers come home," said Hannah. "Martin told Mother and me that Admiral de Grasse's navy has sailed into the Chesapeake. With the French sealing off Cornwallis, we're sure to win."

"I hope you're right," said Lizzie. "I think about my father all the time."

"Have you heard from him?" Hannah asked. The last time she had seen Mr. Reston, the dashing cavalry officer, was about three years ago. He'd been wearing a blue jacket with white straps across his chest, a brass helmet with a red plume, and shiny boots. He'd given her a good-bye salute from the saddle of a spirited white horse.

"He's with Colonel Lee's Legion," said Lizzie, her face darkening. "We haven't received a letter for a long time. Mother pretends she isn't worried, but I know she is." Lizzie straightened a skirt ruffle. "I am too," she confessed.

"It's hard for soldiers to write," Hannah said, reassuringly. "And I'm sure that not all letters can be smuggled in." She lay back and looked at the sky.

"You're probably right, Hannah." Lizzie smiled. "You always know the right thing to say." She lay back in the grass. "I hope our families never leave Yorktown. I don't know what I'd do without you."

Hannah sat up. "I have a wonderful idea!" she said, removing the silver ring she'd been wearing for the past two years. She held it out. "Lizzie, I want you to have this. It's a friendship ring." Lizzie took the ring and slid it onto her third finger. "Now we'll always be friends no matter what happens."

Lizzie removed the gold ring her grandmother had given her, and offered it to Hannah. "And this is for you. I'll never forget you, Hannah."

Hannah slipped the ring on her finger. It fit perfectly. The two friends hugged each other. Then reluctantly, Lizzie pulled away. "It's late," she said. "We'd better start back."

They put on their stockings and shoes, and began their walk home. As they neared Lizzie's house, Hannah was surprised to see Mr. and Mrs. Langtry, Pastor Benson, and Martin standing on the front porch. *Something's wrong*, she thought, her pulse quickening along with her step. Maybe they'd found out Lizzie had snuck down to the river. Having the same thought as Hannah, Lizzie raced ahead.

Mrs. Reston opened the door and, with teary eyes and open arms, ran to meet Lizzie. "Oh my darling! It's your father!" Mrs. Reston's voice cracked.

"Father?" Lizzie touched her mother's cheek.

"Yes!" her mother sobbed. "Martin just brought the letter."

Martin stepped forward, gently placing his hand on Lizzie's shoulder. "I'm sorry, Miss Elizabeth," he said hoarsely. "Your father was missing in action after the Battle of Guilford Courthouse. It happened months ago, but only recently was his death confirmed by two of his comrades. They said he acted bravely and died a heroic death there."

Lizzie's blue eyes clouded with pain and bewilderment. She turned to Hannah, who hugged her close, resting her dry cheek against Lizzie's wet one. "I'm sorry, Lizzie. Truly sorry."

"Come inside, Elizabeth." Lizzie's mother took her daughter's hand and tenderly led her toward the house.

Hannah watched them sadly. Lizzie's mother was so sad she didn't even notice Lizzie's damp, wrinkled dress.

Before entering the house, Lizzie turned toward

Hannah and waved good-bye, her face streaked with tears.

Hannah watched the door close. She had been so light and happy a few moments ago, and now she felt only a heavy sorrow. Poor Lizzie. What would she do? To think her father would never be coming home! How terrible. She felt sympathy for her friend, and hot tears burned her eyes. She kissed the ring Lizzie had given her. Once again, she remembered Mr. Reston's salute as he had ridden away. The memory tore at her heart, and for the first time, dark doubts engulfed her. *Was Father safe? Or was he also lying dead on a battlefield?*

CHAPTER THREE
Hannah to the Rescue

FOR THE NEXT TWO WEEKS HANNAH HAD great difficulty falling asleep. She was certainly aware that many soldiers in the Continental Army had lost their lives, but the death of Lizzie's father hit harder and was far more personal for Hannah. *Why did Mr. Reston have to die?*

One morning after a particularly restless sleep, she woke to the whining sound of the spinning wheel.

"Good morning, Hannah," her mother said from across the room. She was working the shaft on the spinning wheel.

"'Morning," Hannah murmured. She wished she could turn over and try to sleep, but her mother would not tolerate that.

"I'd like you to weed the garden this morning," her mother said, straightening a thread caught in her spinning wheel. "And while you're outside, could you pick a bushel of apples, dear?"

Hannah groaned. She was sick and tired of doing household chores. She rolled out of her trundle bed and smoothed the muslin sheets.

She picked up the china pitcher and filled the wash basin with water. Then she washed her face and hands. The cold water felt refreshing. She pulled on a coarse linen dress, and tied on the white apron she always wore when she did her chores. Then she and her mother walked outside to the kitchen.

Mrs. Winslow had already prepared breakfast. To Hannah's surprise, the salted fish and hot wheat bread tasted good. "Martin says the American troops are beginning to arrive at Williamsburg. I hope we hear from Father soon," she said to her mother.

"It's hard to believe your father is only twelve miles away. But as long as British troops occupy Yorktown, it might as well be a thousand," Mrs. Winslow said.

Hannah jumped up and kissed her mother on her cheek. "With the French navy here, and the army soon to be, the war will soon be over. Father will be coming home."

"I hope so, Hannah." Mrs. Winslow sighed. "Unlike poor Mr. Reston."

"You'd better start weeding the garden before the sun is too high," said Mrs. Winslow, starting to clear the table.

Hannah went out into the garden. Weeds sprouted everywhere—especially among the neat rows of beans. Had they sprouted overnight? She rolled up her sleeves, and took off her bonnet. But the last thing she wanted to do was weed. Shading her eyes, she looked up and out over the back fence where daisies and asters bloomed all the way to the York River and beyond. It was a beautiful sight—the river and the distant trees of Gloucester County.

"Where's your bonnet?" Mrs. Winslow stood in the doorway, her brows knitted in disapproval.

"Who cares about my bonnet!" said Hannah. "It makes my head hot."

"Very well," said her mother. "You don't have to wear it, but you must start weeding. We have lots of chores ahead of us."

The house could burn down and her mother wouldn't flee until the housework was done! Hannah thought.

Just as Hannah began to weed, she heard pounding on the front door.

"Who is it?" called her mother, who had gone back inside.

Hannah raced in through the back door and flung the front door open. Martin strode in impatiently.

"Sit down, Martin," said Mrs. Winslow, motioning to a chair.

"There's no time for sitting," Martin said, restlessly. "We must find a way to get information to General Washington."

"Is there anything we can do to assist?" Hannah asked with hope.

How she wished she could help out. But her mother would probably never let her. A young lady's work is spinning a loom or weeding a garden, she often said.

"Yes, there is," said Martin. He removed his cap and wiped his brow with his forearm. "In fact, I'm counting on you, Hannah. If your mother agrees to it. I'm under suspicion and dare not try to leave Yorktown. But the soldiers won't suspect you." Hannah gasped with excitement as she listened to Martin describe her task. "I want you to leave Yorktown and go to Williamsburg—without letting the Redcoats detain you." And tapping a leather pouch around his neck he said, "I want you to take this pouch. In it are descriptions and maps showing positions of British earthworks around Yorktown. These must be delivered to General Washington. No one else must see them."

"Can I go, Mother?" Hannah pleaded. Her mother was silent.

"It won't be easy sneaking through British lines," said Martin. "And you must be alert to British troops on scouting missions all along the road."

Hannah knew that the road to Williamsburg, though it skirted many rivers and creeks, was direct. She tried to imagine herself on the journey Martin was describing.

"Once you arrive at Halfway Ordinary, a horseman will be waiting for you near Burwell's Mill. When you give him the password, 'Valley Forge,' he'll ride you up the road to Williamsburg." Martin looked closely at Hannah. "I have no doubt it will all go smoothly. You're a brave and quick-witted young woman. If we don't help the Continental Army by detailing British troop positions, then the French navy's presence here could be for naught."

Hannah and Martin looked at Mrs. Winslow.

"I . . . I suppose you should go," said Mrs. Winslow, hesitantly, "considering the circumstances. But Hannah, you must be very careful."

"Oh, I will!" shouted Hannah, thrilled beyond belief. Never in a million years would she have dreamed she'd be picked for such an important assignment. To think this could affect the outcome of the war. With trembling fingers, she took the pouch from Martin and slipped it around her neck. Then she tucked it inside her dress.

Mrs. Winslow grasped Hannah's wrist. "My husband's already in the army," she whispered. "Must I be prepared to sacrifice my daughter, too?"

Martin gently removed Mrs. Winslow's hand. "Please, Maude, let Hannah go. This information could mean a lot to your husband."

"I hope you're right, Martin," said Mrs. Winslow. "I'll pack food and clothes."

"There's no time," said Martin. "Some bread in both pockets will be enough. And she'll have plenty of water from the creeks. It's important that Hannah mustn't arouse suspicion. It should only take her a day."

"Pegg's in Williamsburg," said Hannah, trying to calm her mother's nerves. "She'll give me a change of clothes once I've delivered the maps."

Mrs. Winslow nodded.

Martin went on to give Hannah instructions, making sure she understood exactly where the rider would be waiting. She already knew how to get to Williamsburg. Since she'd visited Pegg several times before, she was even familiar with the main road's landmarks.

"Hannah." Martin's massive hand fell on her shoulders. "You'd better get started."

Hannah looked at her mother, who had tears in her eyes. "I'll be fine," she said, still unable to believe she was doing this. She hurried out the door.

As SHE WALKED PAST LIZZIE'S house, Hannah wished she could tell her friend her exciting news. But she knew there was no time. Soon she reached the port through the earthwork fortifications at the west end of town. Several hundred yards beyond an entrenchment known as Redoubt Two stood an old apple orchard. Two British soldiers, deep in conversation, were standing guard.

"Halt! What is your business?" the taller one said to Hannah. He lowered his musket.

"I'm going to pick apples," Hannah said, smiling.

"Orders are that no one is to leave town," the British guard said, shaking his head. He seemed annoyed to be interrupted.

Despite her pounding heart, Hannah's smile didn't waver. "I'll only be a few minutes, and I'll be in full sight."

"Not today, lass!" said the shorter guard.

"I'll bring you back a delicious apple," Hannah pleaded.

The shorter guard shrugged and glanced at the taller one. "What's the harm?"

"Oh, go ahead!" said the taller guard. "But be quick about it."

"Thank you, sir." Hannah openly walked to the orchard and began to pick apples. Gradually, she wandered farther and farther from the guards. When she reached the back of the orchard, she glanced back nervously. But the guards had resumed their conversation and apparently had forgotten all about her. She began to move more quickly away from Yorktown when she heard: "Get back here!" Hannah turned to see the guards coming after her.

Panic welled up inside her. Dropping the apples, except for one she had managed to put in the pocket with the bread, she began to run for her life.

CHAPTER FOUR
Betrayed

FRANTICALLY, HANNAH SEARCHED FOR A hiding place among the thick forest of pine trees lining the road. She dashed behind the widest trunk she could find and tried not to breathe.

"Oh, let her go!" she heard one of the soldiers say. "One little girl can't hurt our army." With these words, they turned back.

Relieved, Hannah let her breath out. Just to be safe, she counted to one hundred before starting out again.

The road to Williamsburg was little more than two muddy and sandy wagon wheel ruts. Hannah found it very hard to walk quickly, her feet sinking with every step. She also had to leave the trail whenever British horsemen appeared—which was quite often. Walking through the woods was even more difficult, with so many tree roots, bushes, and thorns. Every so often,

Hannah felt for the pouch, just to be sure it was nestled safely. *If the Redcoats knew what information I'm hiding,* Hannah thought, *they'd hang me from the nearest tree!*

From the position of the sun, Hannah knew it was just after noon. As she made her way through the mud, she smiled to herself. She'd never dreamed an adventure could be as exciting as this one. And to think she would meet George Washington. Maybe she'd even see her father.

Though Williamsburg was only twelve miles away, it seemed as if it were much farther. *That's because I've never even walked part of the way before*, Hannah thought to herself. And last time she'd gone, the road hadn't been crawling with British soldiers.

As Hannah trudged along, the sun dipped deeper into the west. She spent most of her time wending her way through the woods, avoiding open areas, passing many rivers and creeks.

Occasionally, the pine forest on each side of the road gave way to bushy, overgrown old fields. As Hannah moved inland away from the York River, she was reminded of how thirsty she was. Her legs ached from carrying the weight of her muddy shoes, now twice their normal size. She yearned to rest but wanted to reach Halfway Ordinary—where she was to meet the horseman—before it got dark. *Would she be able to find him at night?* For a moment, she panicked, trying to recall the password. *What was it? Oh, yes,* she remembered. *Valley Forge.*

Suddenly, a distant singing filled the air. Whirling about, she spotted a unit of British soldiers about a quarter mile behind her. She dived into the thick undergrowth, scarcely noticing the thorns and twigs scratching her face and hands. She was used to such discomfort by now. She prayed that the approaching troops hadn't spotted her.

As the Redcoats drew nearer, their singing grew louder. Hannah felt her heart beat to the rhythm of their marching boots. She peeked out between the dense branches as they began to march past her. But then an officer bellowed orders allowing his men to rest. With that, the Redcoats relaxed. Some found places to rest under trees, while others stayed in the road talking with one another.

Hannah bit her lip. She needed to keep moving, but now she was stuck until the British moved on. Though Martin had said it could take a whole day, Hannah had hoped to surprise everybody by getting there in a matter of hours. But she hadn't considered the mud, the blocked roads, the runs, and the Redcoats. Dusk was falling, and soon she wouldn't be able to see.

Her muscles throbbed. She ached to shift her weight, but dared not make a noise. *Oh, why did the British have to come along at just this instant?* Finally, at least an hour later, while still dusk, the British officer ordered his men to resume their march.

Hannah waited until they were well out of sight and hearing before she came out of her hiding place and tried to move on—but it was no use. She had waited too long. Dusk quickly turned to complete darkness, and it was as dark as the inside of a well. And hot! Disappointed, she wiped the perspiration from her forehead and sank back on the soggy ground. *The best thing to do is find a safe place to sleep*, she reasoned. *I'll start out at the first sliver of light.* All she could do was hope that the horseman would be at Halfway Ordinary in the morning.

A few feet away, Hannah found a small clearing. After taking a long drink from a nearby creek, she began gathering leaves and twigs. Next, she spread her apron over the pile and sat on her homemade bed. It wasn't as comfortable as her bed at home, but it would do. Hungrily, she took the apple from her pocket and devoured it along with most of the bread. Then she lay down and closed her eyes—but sleep wouldn't come.

A mosquito buzzed in Hannah's ear. When she

brushed it away, a whole swarm of the pesky insects descended on her. She tried to shoo them away, too. Then suddenly, she heard something rustling in the brush! She sat straight up.

Clasping her arms around her knees, Hannah huddled in fear, praying it wasn't a wild animal. But whatever had made the noise was silent now. Covering her face with her handkerchief to keep the insects away, she stretched out again. An owl hooted. Finally, exhausted, she drifted into a restless sleep.

HANNAH AWOKE SHORTLY BEFORE dawn. A pink streak in the eastern sky was the only light around. Everything else was covered in a thick, dark fog. As it grew lighter, she was able to make out the outline of the road. Steam was rising from the ground. Everything seemed still and silent, without a Redcoat in sight. Hannah brushed the leaves and dirt off her dress, tied her apron around her waist, and continued along the trail.

A squirrel skittered across her path. *Probably as hungry as I am*, Hannah thought. Since yesterday's breakfast, she had only eaten the bread her mother had given her and the apple. She picked a handful of wild berries to eat along the way.

By early morning, with the fog still thick, Hannah came to a white wooden fence. Even in the mist, she recognized the windmill that stood next to it. She remembered passing it on her way to visit Pegg, and knew she was only about a quarter mile away from Halfway Ordinary. *What if I can't find the horseman?* she wondered. *Maybe he won't be there to meet me!* She forced herself to think positively.

Ten minutes later, Hannah reached the open pasture behind the stable at the Ordinary. She climbed a rail fence, approaching the little tavern with cautious but determined steps. The misty fog made it hard to see, but suddenly, she heard hoof steps.

"Over here!" she called.

Silence.

"This way!" she shouted. "Valley Forge!"

The sound of hoof steps came closer as Hannah raced toward the tavern. From the right side of the small, red brick house came a dark figure on horseback, trotting towards her.

"Thank God," she whispered. Then in a louder voice she said, "Are you to ride me to Williamsburg?"

"Ye knew the password, didn't ye?" came a man's gruff reply. The horse whinnied as the rider pulled back on its reins.

"I'm Hannah Winslow," Hannah said, heading toward the horse.

"Climb on!" the man ordered harshly. With that, he offered her his hand for assistance.

Carefully, Hannah placed her right foot in the stirrup all the while holding the man's right hand. She swung her left leg over the horse until she was squarely atop, sitting behind her escort.

As soon as she was settled, Hannah leaned out to the side so as to have a look at the horseman. Aside from his long nose and angular jaw, she couldn't see much. Sitting behind him made it impossible to see his eyes. She held onto the man around his waist.

"You're to take me up the road to Williamsburg," she said, trying to keep her voice steady. The horseman didn't answer. *Why is he so grouchy?* Hannah wondered. *After all, he must be a Patriot since he's part of this plan.*

The horseman galloped gracefully further and further up the road.

It won't be long now before I'm safely in the company of the Continental Army, Hannah thought.

"Do you live in Williamsburg?" she asked politely.

"No," the man muttered.

But his curt reply didn't stop Hannah's curiosity. "Then you must live near Yorktown," she said.

"That's none of your business!" the horseman snapped.

Doesn't he know I'm carrying a message for General Washington? Hannah wondered, starting to get angry. Instead of snarling at her, he should be grateful. She decided not to say another word.

The mist, and the constant sound of the hooves, caused Hannah to become frightened. Here she was in the wilderness with an unfriendly stranger! *Why, with one good swat he could knock me right off this horse*, she thought.

Suddenly, the man commanded his stag to stop, allowing the powerful animal to graze on the neat lines of grass along the road.

"Why did you stop?" Hannah asked, puzzled. She took in her surroundings, growing more and more nervous by the second. She noticed the approaching mill dam of Burwell's Mill about fifty yards up the road. "I'm in a hurry. I can't waste a single second. Our army may depend on me." The horseman turned, grabbed Hannah firmly by her forearm, and lowered her down from the horse.

Smiling deviously, he said, "You have information I want." He dismounted and took a step closer to Hannah all in one motion.

Instinctively, Hannah clutched the pouch. "What do you mean?" A sense of cold fear came over her.

"Just give me what you have," he said roughly. Then he lunged at her.

"No!" Hannah shouted, pulling away.

The horseman grasped her arm, his bony fingers digging into her flesh. Hannah struggled to free herself.

"Hand over the information! Now!" the rider demanded.

"Never!" Hannah answered, breathing in short gasps. "Wh-why are you doing this? You're being paid by Americans!"

The horseman's high-pitched laugh chilled her.

"Traitor!" she yelled.

"I'm no traitor," the horseman hissed. "The British just pay more than the Colonials." He grabbed her other arm with his free hand.

Hannah kicked him hard, causing him to lose his grip, and then scampered away, closer to the dam.

"Where do you think you're going?" the horseman sneered. He took a step toward her. And another.

Hannah, paralyzed with fear, stared at him as he moved toward her. "There's nowhere to go, you little biddy," he taunted.

Hannah couldn't allow this awful man to steal her

valuable information. With just a second's hesitation, she ran over to the dam, stepping up onto the dam's dirt wall without breaking stride. In another moment she dived into the mirky water. Down, down, down she plunged, the warm muddy water of the mill pond blotting out the mill, the evil horseman, and the world.

CHAPTER FIVE

Almost Drowned

A S HANNAH SANK DEEPER AND DEEPER, all she could see was darkness. When she could no longer hold her breath, she struggled to the surface, feeling feathery ferns brushing against her legs. Just as she poked her head out, a swift wave came. Her nose filled with water as she tumbled back into the dark depths. *Is this the end?* she wondered. *Will I ever see Mother and Father again? Will I ever see Pegg or Lizzie?*

Again, she fought her way upward. Sputtering, she broke through the surface and breathed in great gulps of air. She felt for the pouch—and couldn't find it! She thought about diving for it, but searching the muddy bottom would be hopeless.

Suddenly, she heard the sound of the horseman's voice. *Was he heading in her direction? Was he now in the pond?* She inhaled as much air as she could, and then dived beneath the murky water. Trying not to splash, she swam underwater in the opposite direction, away from where she thought she heard the voice, finally surfacing a few yards away.

She heard the horseman curse as small stones hit the water fifty feet away. "Where are you, little biddy?" came the familiar, gruff voice. "I'll wait for you. It might take a while, but I have all the time in the world. I won't let you get away!"

The horseman's voice choked Hannah with fear. But she realized that he wasn't in the water, and did not appear to be particularly eager for an early morning dip. *Maybe he can't swim*, Hannah thought. She swam as quickly, and as quietly as she could. Her arms felt like lead, but she just kept swimming! *Surely he must hear me*, she thought, taking comfort in the memory of swimming lessons from her father.

Suddenly, Hannah felt something tugging at her skirt, drawing her underwater again. She kicked with all her might and managed to tear free. *It's only a water plant*, she reassured herself.

Exhausted, Hannah was thankful for the thick fog. She tried to keep her head up, but her chin began to dip into the water. Her legs and arms ached. Forcing her legs to kick, she managed to bob to the surface once more. Coughing and sputtering, she struggled for air. Again she heard the man's voice, but this time it seemed to be farther away. How would she ever find her way to shore?

How could she have lost the precious pouch? The tight leather thong had been secured around her neck. Even if she reached land, she had failed Martin's trust in her. But now, exhausted, she needed to concentrate on surviving. With steady, determined strokes, she swam in search of solid ground. Otherwise, she would drown.

It felt as if she'd been swimming for hours when something brushed across her face. It was a cattail—a sign that she was near the shore. She listened for the familiar gruff voice, but heard nothing. With that, she began to grab the tough cattail stalks, pulling herself toward shallow water. Minutes later, she gasped in pleasant relief as she could touch bottom.

Hannah waded through the shallow water. When she reached the shore, she collapsed on the small beach, trying to catch her breath. Somehow she had escaped her assailant. *He must have tired of the chase*, Hannah reasoned.

But she still had a mission to carry out. Painfully, she hauled herself up and felt around for the leather pouch. Her sodden dress was draped in clumps of seaweed—but there was no pouch. It must have sunk to the bottom of Burwell's Mill Pond. Her mission had ended in failure.

Miserably, Hannah tried to decide what to do. Should

she return home? If she did, how would she ever be able to face Martin? No, she had to go on. Maybe she could go see General Washington anyway. She could tell him the truth—that she'd lost the information at Burwell's Mill. But if he asked her the precise location of Cornwallis's troops, what would she say? Martin hadn't told her the specifics.

With no time to lose, she pulled a clump of seaweed from her legs. *Why did the seaweed feel so heavy? Could it be?* She ripped the seaweed apart, and there, nestled in the center, was the leather pouch. "Thank you," she whispered softly, and carefully hid the pouch in her pocket. Then she hurried through the brush alongside the road to Williamsburg.

As she walked, Hannah wondered if Pegg would be happy to see her. They had never been close, never shared secrets the way she and Lizzie had. Maybe it was because Pegg was six years older. She remembered a spring day when she had won a spelling bee held at her tutor's. Several other children in Yorktown had been invited to participate. Her victory was earned by spelling *scissors* correctly. When she got home, she eagerly showed Pegg her prize: a book of Greek mythology. Instead of being proud of her younger sister, Pegg had told her spelling wasn't important for young ladies. Instead, she should spend more time at the loom. From that day on, Hannah taught herself to read, though Pegg and her mother thought her time would be better spent doing household chores.

As the fog lifted, Hannah began to recognize the farmhouses around her. Knowing she was close to Williamsburg, Hannah felt a new burst of energy and was able to quicken her step. As she neared the village, the road became wider and smoother to accommodate carriages as well as wagons. Since she didn't see any Redcoats, she began to feel safer.

Soon Hannah saw sunlight reflecting off a cupola in the distance. Although she was still more than two miles from town, she recognized it as the old colonial capitol. *"I've made it!"* she thought, proudly.

AS HANNAH NEARED WILLIAMSBURG, she slowed to a walk. Her damp dress clung to her. Her shoes, wet and tight, squished when she ran. But she barely noticed. How pleased General George Washington would be to receive her news. Oh, how she wished Lizzie could share this adventure! She smiled down at the ring Lizzie had given her, and was glad they had made the exchange before her departure.

Suddenly, she heard a movement in the bushes. She tried to race ahead—but it was too late. A British soldier dashed forward and grabbed her.

"Where are you going in such a rush, my fair maiden?" said the Redcoat, a strong, thickset man, his grip tight on Hannah's forearm.

"Let me go or I'll scream," said Hannah, trying to twist free.

The Redcoat laughed, clapping a hand over her mouth. "I don't think you'll utter a sound." He tightened his grip. "Tell me, why are you in such a hurry? Maybe you're hiding information!"

"I'm not," Hannah said, hoping he couldn't see the bulge in her apron pocket. "I-I'm on my way to my sister's house." She tried to steady her trembling hands, determined to outwit him. She wasn't going to let him interfere with her meeting with General Washington.

"Is that so?" the soldier asked suspiciously. "Why, I just met up with one of our hired couriers a few miles back. He warned all British scouts to be on the lookout for a frightened and wet fair maiden. If you tell me what you're hiding, I'll let you go."

"All-all right," she stammered, trying to think her way out of this. "I . . ."

"Where are you from?" interrupted the Redcoat.

"I'm from Williamsburg," she lied, with a boldness she didn't feel.

He looked her up and down. "There's something

fishy about you, and it isn't just the smell!" He laughed at his own joke. "From the looks of it, you went for a swim in Burwell's Mill Pond."

Hannah pushed back a damp curl. "My foot slipped and I fell into the dam," she explained.

The soldier studied Hannah's face, unsure whether or not to believe her. "I think my commanding officer would like to talk to you," he said, nodding slowly. "Let's go, little lass. We'll head back to Yorktown. I'll leave the scouting of French and American lines to my comrades."

Hannah's heart sank. How could she return to Yorktown after she had finally reached the outskirts of Williamsburg? "My sister will worry if I'm not home for dinner," she said.

"Sorry, my lass, but you're coming with me," the soldier said sternly.

Just then, they heard the sound of marching and singing. It was a regiment of Continental soldiers, coming up the road.

Continental soldiers! Hannah's heart leapt with joy. She tried to break free and yell for help, but the Redcoat covered her mouth and quickly forced her off the road into the dense brush. The loud singing would have drowned out any cry Hannah could manage, anyway.

As the singing faded into the distance, the Redcoat

loosened his grip. "It's back to Yorktown with you!"

Hannah couldn't believe her bad luck. She'd been within shouting distance of her allies.

"Come along," the soldier said, dragging her back onto the road.

Hannah refused to go willingly. The thought of returning to Yorktown made her miserable. A wave of panic swept over her when she thought of the pouch. She must think of a way to destroy the maps. If the British discovered that she was a messenger, she'd be hanged as a spy.

They'd only gone a few yards when a unit of French horsemen approached. Again the British soldier forced Hannah off the road and into the brush.

This was her last chance. Hannah kicked the Redcoat, bit his hand, and yelled, "Help!"

"Owww!" the Redcoat squealed in pain. He pushed Hannah aside and, not wanting to face the French horsemen alone, ran as fast as his heavy legs would carry him.

Catching her breath, Hannah almost felt sorry for the Redcoat, but she couldn't waste time thinking about him. She had an important mission to carry out. Only a few days before, she'd been thrilled about this trip. But after dodging Redcoats, escaping from a horrible horseman, and swimming in the pond, Hannah hoped there would be no more obstacles. *What else could possibly happen to her?*

CHAPTER SIX
Hannah Meets George Washington

HANNAH CONTINUED ON HER WAY, half stumbling, half-running, she rushed through a cornfield. After she emerged from the tall stalks she came upon what appeared to be an American encampment. Hundreds of soldiers were milling about, some laughing and joking with one another, others just resting.

It didn't take long for Hannah to notice that they were not speaking English. *Could they be General Lafayette's men?* she wondered. Just as she was taking in this impressive sight, she was tapped from behind on her shoulder.

"Je m'excuse," a sentry uttered. Though Hannah didn't understand what he said, it was clear he did not mean to frighten her.

"Please," Hannah said with a pained expression on her face, "I have an urgent message for General Washington."

"*Je ne comprends pas,*" said the sentry. It was just her luck! The first allied soldier she'd met on her journey to Williamsburg couldn't speak English. "Please," said the sentry through a thick French accent as he motioned for Hannah to come with him.

As she accompanied him through the camp, Hannah became something of a spectacle. Young girls—disheveled or otherwise—were not common sights amid military encampments. Just the same, Hannah tried to remain as calm and inconspicuous as possible. After all, she still had an important mission to carry out.

Within a minute or two, the sentry brought her to another soldier who promptly exchanged remarks in French with the sentry. He then looked at Hannah very closely, raising his eyebrows at her soggy, mud-caked appearance.

"I am Sergeant Beaudette of the First Brigade of General Lafayette's Light Infantry," he announced in English. "Who are you and what is your business here? The wilderness is no place for a young girl when there is a war going on—unless she is a spy." His accent was thick, but his English clear and his manner courteous.

"If you please, Sergeant Beaudette," came a rather timid reply from Hannah, "my name is Hannah Winslow and I *am* spying—for the Americans."

She took the pouch out of her pocket and handed it to the sergeant. The sergeant unfolded the maps and charts and began to study them.

"These show British troop positions around Yorktown," said Hannah, starting to gain a good deal more confidence.

"*Hmm, c'est magnifique,*" said the French trooper as he scrutinized all of the papers.

From his reaction Hannah felt a sense of optimism she had not known since her ordeal began. *Was she finally going into Williamsburg to meet the general?* In another moment she got her answer as she watched Sergeant Beaudette issue several sets of instructions to different men.

"Thank you, Sergeant Beaudette."

Within minutes another French trooper approached Hannah and the sergeant riding a horse-drawn wagon. After the driver stopped, the two men helped Hannah into the wagon where the driver returned the pouch to her. He nodded politely as she sat beside him on the bench. With that Hannah was once again on her way to Williamsburg.

As the wagon plodded onward toward the town, Hannah and her escort passed other encampments along the way. Hannah marveled at the handsome, white uniforms the French wore. And each time the two arrived at a military camp, the driver brought the wagon to a halt so he could state his business to the sentry. Each time, the wagon was allowed to pass with little delay.

After about fifteen minutes from the time she left Sergeant Beaudette, Hannah arrived within the confines of Williamsburg. They trotted down its main thoroughfare, Duke of Gloucester Street, where Hannah's attention was immediately drawn to the colonial capital. Dozens of soldiers were moving tables and cots into the building.

"*L'hôpital,*" Hannah's escort said, noticing her puzzled look at the commotion.

The capital is to be used as a makeshift hospital, Hannah thought. She became chilled at the thought that a hospital would soon be necessary.

The tantalizing smell of fresh baked bread wafting from Raleigh Tavern off to her right reminded her of her empty stomach. How she yearned to stop and eat. Though droves of soldiers and civilians alike were coming and going into the tavern, Hannah resolved that she was just going to have to wait.

As they continued along Duke of Gloucester Street Hannah noticed a few small stores, sometimes with the store merchants standing out front. Other buildings had become very run-down. But nothing stood out as much as the abandoned buildings. There was no doubt in Hannah's mind that the war exacted a terrible price on the inhabitants of Williamsburg.

Hannah wanted to take everything in, but the hardship she witnessed forced her to look down in hopes of blocking out her painful surroundings. She looked at her hands. Dusty palms and mud beneath the fingernails reminded her of how much she needed a bath. She thought about asking her escort to take her to a well so she could rinse off. General Washington deserved her respect. But not wanting to waste any more time, she decided against it.

As they approached Market Square, Hannah noticed the courthouse on the right and the Public Magazine on her left where troops appeared to retrieve various supplies. *Oh, what effort this war takes,* Hannah mused.

She looked back to her right. Just behind the courthouse she noticed a company of soldiers, bearing muskets, marching back and forth. The troops were drilling under the instructions of a wide-shouldered officer. Hannah wondered if it were the famous German commander, Baron Von Steuben, who had trained the Continental Army at Valley Forge. Her question was answered when she heard a messenger call his name.

Hannah's escort kept the wagon going west until they reached the foot of Palace Green where he pulled the reins to the right, guiding the horse in that direction. Now all of the landmarks Hannah remembered from her earlier visits with Pegg came into full view. There was the Governor's Palace at the end of the Green, Bruton Parish Church to her left, and of course, George Wythe's impressive home on the western side of Palace Green. *But somehow, everything looked different now. Was it the war, or all that Hannah had just been through?* She just wasn't sure.

The French soldier steered the wagon up to George Wythe's home. Apparently this was George Washington's temporary headquarters. Hannah felt her heart begin to race.

After tying the reins to a nearby post, the escort hurried to the front door. Hannah followed closely behind. "What's all the noise?" said an irritated voice from inside, an apparent response to the persistent knocking. When the door opened, Hannah was face-to-face with an aide staring down at her. "What in the world . . ."

With a polite nod to the French soldier, the aide dismissed him, before quickly returning his stare at Hannah.

Does he think I'm a witch? Hannah wondered, knowing

she must look like one. With her hair hanging about her face in tangled knots and her torn and dirty clothes, it was no wonder the aide looked horrified. Maybe she should have found a well first. Her mother would be humiliated if she knew her daughter was in George Washington's headquarters with a dirty face and shoes caked with mud. Hannah hoped the General would excuse her appearance once she had given him the information.

"I must see General Washington," she said, as calmly as she could. "I have a vital message for him."

The aide rubbed his chin doubtfully, sizing her up.

"Please, sir," Hannah pleaded, "I've come all the way from Yorktown."

"Very well," said the soldier. "The General is resting, but I'll tell him you're here." He hesitated, as if he weren't sure this were the right thing to do. "What's your name?"

"Hannah Winslow," Hannah responded promptly.

The soldier escorted her into a large room, and scurried upstairs.

Hannah sighed with relief. *At last!* She pushed back a strand of hair and tried to smooth her wrinkled skirt. She hoped no one would notice the mud she'd tracked inside. She removed the leather pouch and held it tightly.

As she waited, she glanced about the huge room. A

round table strewn with maps and charts was surrounded by ten chairs. There was also a slant-topped desk, a red sandstone fireplace, a wooden chess set, and a spinet piano.

Suddenly, Hannah felt a wave of exhaustion. She had been so excited that she'd forgotten how tired she was. Her legs felt weak and her eyes felt heavy. She certainly couldn't fall asleep now. Then an awful thought struck her: *What if General Washington won't see me?* A wave of dizziness swept over her. She grasped the back of a chair to steady herself.

She heard footsteps coming down the stairs. The aide hurried into the room followed by an exceptionally tall soldier. This soldier was a gentleman from the peak of his forehead to the bottom of his polished boots. His uniform with its high white collar was exquisite.

Unsmiling, the man observed Hannah with the bluest eyes she'd ever seen, steady, but not unkind. "I'm George Washington, Miss Winslow. What can I do for you?"

"I-I've come from Yorktown," Hannah stammered, his steady gaze unnerving her. He didn't seem to mind her bedraggled appearance. With trembling hands, she offered him the pouch.

With long deft fingers, the General opened the pouch and pulled out Martin's information. His aide helped him unfold the parchment and spread it on the table.

General Washington picked up the parchment, studying it closely. "This shows the position of British troops in Yorktown," he said, nodding with approval. "There's no escape for Cornwallis now!" He turned to his aide. "We shall plot our strategy tonight at dinner when Generals Lafayette and Rochambeau arrive. We shall march to Yorktown as soon as possible."

He swung around to face Hannah. "Good work, Hannah Winslow." For the first time, he noticed her dirty dress. "Have you been dunked in one of the creeks?" he asked, with a twinkle in his eyes. "Would you like a woman servant to bathe you?" the General asked.

"Th-thank you, sir, but no," said Hannah. "My sister lives nearby. I can get cleaned up there." The happiness flowing through her was worth every hardship she had gone through. General Washington was actually holding Martin's map in his hands.

Suddenly, she felt very lightheaded. She tried to grab the back of a chair to steady herself, but she didn't make it in time. Everything went black.

CHAPTER SEVEN
Pegg

HANNAH OPENED HER EYES TO FIND General Washington gazing down at her. "Are you all right?" he asked.

"Yes, sir," she replied, embarrassed at her show of weakness.

"Sergeant Everly," he said to the aide, "please fetch a piece of chicken and a glass of milk for Miss Winslow." Then, he turned back to Hannah, and he held out his hand. "Come with me."

In awe, Hannah allowed General Washington to lead her into the dining room. The white linen table-cloth was set with fine china and crystal. Apparently Washington was entertaining the French generals in style. A vase full of asters and marigolds stood in the center of the table, a tall candle on each side. The floral carpet felt thick and soft beneath her feet.

Once she was seated and the food set before her, the general sat down beside her. "You're a brave girl, Hannah," he said. "You've done a great service to your country."

Hannah was speechless. Not only had General George Washington held her hand, but he had called her a *brave girl!* The General smiled at her, and left her to devour the meal.

When Hannah had finished every last morsel, she looked around her. She glanced out the red-draped window, astonished to see the setting sun. The day, crammed with one event after another, had flown by.

"Would you like to rest, Miss Winslow?" Startled, Hannah turned to see Sergeant Everly.

"No, thank you. As I told General Washington, sir, I'd like to stay with my sister, Pegg Isley. She lives here in Williamsburg on Francis Street."

The sergeant looked at her sympathetically. "You look pale and tired and," he added with a smile, "dirty."

"I am." Hannah giggled. "But I feel much better now that I have eaten."

"Very well," said the sergeant. "You shall be escorted to your sister's home. In the meantime, I'll send word back to Mr. Jamison, informing him that his maps have been delivered. We'll request he tell your mother that you are safe and sound." He motioned for Hannah to follow him, and led her out the front door where another soldier waited. "Corporal, take Miss Winslow to Francis Street. She has been a great help to our cause."

"Yes, sir," the corporal said, with a salute.

Sergeant Everly shook Hannah's hand. "It's been an honor to meet you. You won't be forgotten."

Hannah smiled as she descended the front steps along with her escort. It had taken her nearly two days to go twelve miles. If there hadn't been a war going on, she could have done it in six hours.

When Hannah and her new escort reached Francis Street, Hannah pointed to Pegg's house. "It's the one with the carved pineapple above the door." She remembered when her father had presented that pineapple, symbol of hospitality, to Pegg and David. He had carved it for them himself. The soldier waited until she reached the front door before bidding Hannah a polite good-bye.

For a moment, she stood with her hand on the knocker. *Would Pegg welcome her?* Her heart raced as she let the knocker drop.

The door opened. "Hannah!" cried Pegg, pulling her younger sister inside. "What happened to you?

Why are you here?"

"It's a long story, Pegg," said Hannah, "but right now, I'm too tired to talk."

"But look at you, Hannah! Your clothes are a mess, your hair is tangled, and you have dark circles around your eyes."

"I know," Hannah murmured, looking at her older sister. Even in an apron, with a towel slung across her shoulder, Pegg looked dainty and neat. Her brown hair was pulled back in a knot, and her pretty face was as pale as ever. Hannah felt dirty and awkward next to Pegg— but right now, she just had to get some sleep.

"Sit down, Hannah, and I'll draw a bath for you," Pegg said, matter-of-factly. She spread the towel across the wing-back chair, and motioned for Hannah to sit on it.

Hannah dropped into the chair. As Pegg began unfastening her shoes, Hannah closed her eyes. "These boots are ruined, but don't worry. I have a pair that will fit you." Hannah nodded.

"Why are you in Williamsburg?" Pegg asked, in a puzzled voice.

Wriggling her toes in contentment, Hannah opened her eyes. "I delivered a message to General Washington."

"To *George* Washington!" Pegg cried.

Hannah smiled. "I'll tell you everything later," she

promised, "if you'll just let me sleep."

"Very well," said Pegg. "But first, you must take off *all* your clothes and throw them in the hamper. I'll get you a clean nightgown. When you awaken, you can take a hot bath."

Hannah pulled herself out of the chair, and wearily followed Pegg up the stairs. It was good to see Pegg, and though all she wanted was to sleep, she loved the attention her sister was giving her.

The beautiful four-poster bed in the guest room looked heavenly. Hannah's muscles ached as she removed her clothes. Pegg helped her slip a soft white nightgown over her head. Then she climbed into the bed and Pegg tucked her in, thrusting a down pillow under her head. The feather mattress was much softer than the hard ground she had slept on the night before.

"Now," Pegg said gently, "sleep as late as . . ." But Hannah was asleep before she heard the rest of Pegg's sentence.

HANNAH AWOKE TO SUNLIGHT streaming through the windows. She rolled over, uncertain as to where she was. Oh yes, how could she forget? She was in Pegg's guest room. She glanced down at the white nightgown, amazed that Pegg had permitted her to wear it before she took a bath. What luxury! She yawned and stretched.

The door opened a crack and Pegg peeked in at her. "I see the sleepyhead has finally opened her eyes," she said, entering with a cup of coffee.

"Yes, and I feel wonderful!" Hannah said, laughing.

Pegg wore a white ruffled cap, a matching white apron, and brown dress, looking as neat as usual. She gave Hannah the tea and smiled.

"So, what is this about General George Washington?" Pegg asked, sitting on the edge of the bed.

Hannah related the story of Martin's maps, her scare at Burwell's Mill, and how she'd finally reached the General.

"Hannah, you're a heroine," Pegg marveled. "I'm so proud of you!"

"I'm just happy to be here," Hannah said, basking in Pegg's praise. She'd never thought of herself as a heroine before.

"A sad thing happened, though," Hannah said, sounding serious. She felt guilty that Lizzie had been out of her thoughts for much of the past two days.

"What's that?" Pegg asked, her smile disappearing.

"Lizzie's father was killed at Guilford Courthouse,"

Hannah answered quietly.

"I'm sorry," Pegg answered regretfully. For a moment their silence was broken only by a cart rattling by.

"I've filled the tub with water," Pegg said, touching Hannah's hand. "When you're ready, come downstairs for a good scrubbing."

Hannah had hoped for breakfast first, but a bath sounded good, too.

After she had finished her coffee, Hannah went downstairs. Pegg's home was lovely. Everything was in its place, and all the furniture was polished to a fine sheen. Before he had been called up to service in the Virginia militia, David had practiced law, and could afford to give Pegg expensive furniture and other luxuries. And not only did Pegg know how to manage such a home, but also how to fit in with the ladies of Williamsburg. Hannah glanced into the parlor. The marble fireplace, jade settee, two wing-back chairs, and a crimson carpet gave the room a cozy feeling.

Hannah followed Pegg's voice to a small room. There, Pegg stood next to a round wooden tub. She held a thick sponge, reminding Hannah of a warrior ready for battle.

Hannah stepped into the tub, and sank slowly into the warm soapy water. *Ahhh*, she thought, closing her eyes, *this is heaven*. But when Pegg began to scour her back and neck, her eyes flew open. *This isn't heaven! Pegg scrubs awfully hard. I guess I need it*, Hannah thought, trying her best to bear it. Once Hannah had been scrubbed and scoured from head to toe, Pegg helped her out of the large basin and handed her a towel. "I'm not finished with you yet," she said.

"What next?" Hannah asked, watching her sister pour the filthy water into the yard, before rinsing and refilling the tub with clean water.

"Now, for your hair," Pegg said, lowering Hannah's head into the water. Using her fingers, Pegg massaged soap into Hannah's scalp. Next, she rinsed Hannah's hair with vinegar and water.

"Ooooh!" Hannah wailed. "That stings."

"Now, we're finished," Pegg said, starting to dry Hannah's auburn curls with a towel. "Your hair is really clean."

With her head in a towel wrapped turban-style, Hannah sniffed. "What's that I smell?" she asked, hungrily.

"Freshly baked bread," Pegg said, motioning Hannah to sit in a wooden chair.

Hannah sat down, and Pegg served her porridge and bread. Every mouthful tasted delicious. Just as Hannah finished her second helping, Pegg left the room. Seconds later, she was back, holding a comb and brush. "Time to comb out your snarls," she said.

Hannah groaned, knowing the pulling and tugging would hurt. "It'll be worth every tug to have shiny hair with no tangles," said Pegg, reading Hannah's mind.

Dutifully, Hannah followed her sister outside to the back steps. She sat with her back to Pegg so she could comb through each knot. Each painful yank brought tears to Hannah's eyes. "I'm sorry," Pegg said, "but I need to get the tangles out." After several minutes, the comb slid more easily through Hannah's curls. Pegg put down the comb, and stroked Hannah's hair until it fell softly about her shoulders. Then, she handed Hannah a mirror.

Hannah grinned, pleased at what she saw. She touched her thick auburn curls, softer and silkier than when she combed them herself.

"Now, you look presentable," said Pegg, approvingly. "You know, you've grown into such a pretty young lady. A year makes quite a difference!"

Hannah smiled with surprise. She couldn't remember Pegg ever giving her a compliment on her appearance before. She looked in the mirror again. Was she really pretty?

Pegg laughed, taking away the mirror. "Don't be so vain, Hannah!"

Hannah laughed with her. She couldn't wait to tell Lizzie that Pegg had been so nice to her. Thinking about Lizzie reminded her that she ought to be getting back. Her mother and Martin would be anxious to hear about her mission.

"What are you thinking about?" asked Pegg.

"Home," said Hannah. "Even though I'm having a nice time with you, I should be getting home soon."

"Home?" Pegg echoed. "But you can't leave Williamsburg. With the army about to march there, civilians aren't allowed to go into Yorktown. You'll stay here until we know it's safe to travel."

Hannah felt her heart drop. "But what am I going to do here?" she asked, feeling trapped.

"There's plenty of work to be done," Pegg said.

"Work?" said Hannah. "Your house looks like you do, Pegg—neat, clean, and beautiful."

"I didn't mean housework," said Pegg. "Follow me."

Hannah followed Pegg into the dining room, which looked nothing like she remembered. Last time she was there, a gleaming mahogany table had been set with pewter dinner plates, tall silver candlesticks, and a porcelain vase filled with flowers. Now, the table, covered with a heavy cloth, was heaped with soldiers' uniforms.

"It's mending time," said Pegg, sitting down and opening her sewing kit. "Have a seat, Hannah."

Miserably, Hannah sank into a chair, accepting the thread and needle that Pegg handed her. She hated sewing, and Pegg knew it. She'd much rather be out-doors, wading in a river or running through a field of flowers. Anything but sitting and stitching for hours.

"All these trousers and jackets need repair," Pegg said, picking up a jacket. "Sergeant Jones brings a wag-onload every Monday."

"You know how crooked my stitches are," Hannah said, hoping Pegg would reconsider.

Pegg gave her a small smile. "I don't think a soldier will mind if his patch isn't sewn straight," Pegg said, smiling. "It's the least you can do to help our troops, Hannah."

Pegg was right, of course. Feeling guilty, Hannah began to mend a vest. Just the same, she couldn't think of a worse way to spend an afternoon.

"Six of my neighbors join me every Monday and Wednesday," said Pegg. "Mending's more fun when you have company."

"What day is this?" Hannah asked.

"Thursday," Pegg said, raising her eyebrows. "Have

you lost track of time? Thursday, September 27th—to be precise."

"I guess I have," said Hannah. Had she only left on Tuesday morning? It seemed like more than a month ago. "Ow!" Hannah sucked on her finger. "Stupid needle."

"You'll never make a seamstress, Hannah," Pegg said, disapprovingly.

"I don't want to be a seamstress!" Hannah glared at Pegg. "There are more important things in this world than sewing."

"Like what? Dodging Redcoats and delivering word of enemy positions to generals?" Pegg folded the jacket she'd been working on and reached for another. "I declare, Hannah, don't you think it's time you outgrew your boisterous ways?"

"I intend to help," Hannah snapped. Less than an hour ago, they'd been having such a nice time. What had happened? "Isn't there something else I can do?" Hannah pleaded.

"I suppose you can roll bandages," said Pegg.

THE NEXT MORNING AFTER breakfast, Hannah joined Pegg in the dining room. The room looked oddly empty.

"Good morning, Hannah," Pegg said, smiling with

approval at Hannah's clean dress and brushed-back curls. "I just heard that our army is leaving Williamsburg."

"Wonderful!" shouted Hannah, with shining eyes. "That must have been what I heard earlier this morning—all those wagons and soldiers passing by the window." She grabbed her sister's hand. "Pegg, does this mean Washington will try to overrun Cornwallis?"

"Yes, it does," said Pegg. "Sergeant Jones picked up the mended uniforms just a few minutes ago. He's hurrying to join his division on the march to Yorktown."

"I knew the room looked different," said Hannah. "The uniforms are gone." Hannah was surprised to feel a pang of disappointment, having realized that she'd been looking forward to sewing with Pegg today. Despite her sore, needle-poked fingers, sewing with Pegg had proved to be a peaceful chore. Hannah and Pegg had grown much closer since Hannah's arrival, and she was no longer as eager to return to Yorktown as she had been a couple of days ago.

CHAPTER EIGHT
Back to Yorktown

AS THE NEXT COUPLE OF DAYS PASSED, Hannah helped Pegg with a variety of chores: sewing, knitting, rolling bandages, making lye soap and candles from melted fat, weeding the herb garden, spinning wool, washing clothes, and cooking.

In addition to keeping a beautiful home, Pegg was also a wonderful cook, having learned how to make partridge pie, stews, and cakes from her mother. Hannah didn't care much about cooking, but she sure liked eating a good meal. Maybe someday she would meet someone for whom she would want to cook. Who could tell what the future would bring?

She knew her mother longed for her to come home. She and Pegg had received a note from her since Hannah's arrival. Earlier, Martin had received the message from Sergeant Everly, and passed it on to

Mrs. Winslow.

Hannah had never realized how important Martin's job was until she'd been away. As an American spy in Yorktown, he brought letters from American soldiers to their loved ones almost every day. And if he hadn't told Mrs. Winslow that Hannah was safe, her mother would be sick with worry. Hannah smiled at the thought of seeing her mother and Lizzie. She touched Lizzie's gold ring.

Hearing a loud rumbling from the road, Hannah trotted outside. Troops in formation paraded by, while artillery wagons rumbled along beside them. When Hannah noticed the American flag with its thirteen stripes and stars on a blue field, her heartbeat quickened. *Were the colonies about to be free?*

All day long, she and Pegg sat on the front steps watching the parade. The rat-a-tat of drums brought the feeling of exhilaration to all of Williamsburg.

By late afternoon, the last cart and the last soldier had disappeared. The sudden silence gave the town a strange, haunting sensation. Hannah gazed at the empty road, the road that would eventually take her home!

DURING THE NEXT TWO WEEKS the sisters grew much closer than they had ever been before. Hannah had finally seen the lighter, more easygoing side of Pegg. Whether Hannah brought it out in Pegg, she couldn't say for sure. But one thing she was certain of: when the war finally ended, and they resumed their normal lives, Hannah was going to miss these days the two of them had shared.

On the other hand, the sisters were not similarly optimistic about the progress of the war. "Remember, Hannah, Cornwallis won't surrender without a fight," Pegg said. "We haven't won the war yet."

"But we will," Hannah insisted.

"You're being too optimistic," said Pegg. "Look at both sides of the picture, and be prepared for the worst! Then you won't end up disappointed."

"I believe with all my heart that Washington's troops will defeat Cornwallis," said Hannah. But then she thought back to Guilford Courthouse, the battle where poor Lizzie's father had been killed. The British had fought desperately, and although Cornwallis had lost a quarter of his army, he'd kept attacking.

Pegg was right. The British could fight like tigers. Maybe she shouldn't be so confident that the Americans would prevail. But it was much easier to think positively. She was different from Pegg—and she promised herself to stay optimistic. *General Washington just had to win!*

"I should fix dinner," said Pegg. She looked tired.

"Let me," Hannah suggested. "I'll bake an apple pie." When Pegg looked at her doubtfully, she quickly added, "You've taught me so much, Pegg. Let me show you what I've learned." She leapt up and impulsively kissed Pegg on the forehead. "I'll do the wash later, too. I promise."

Suddenly, a thunderous boom was heard off in the distance. Both girls gasped.

"What was that?" Hannah asked fearfully, her fingers clutching the edge of the table.

"It has to be cannon," said Pegg. "Washington's troops must be bombarding the British in Yorktown."

"But Yorktown is twelve miles away!" said Hannah.

"Cannon can be very loud," said Pegg.

"Oh no," Hannah said, her voice trembling. "Will Mother be safe?"

"I'm sure she will," Pegg said, biting her lower lip. "Before David joined his militia company, he assured me that when this day arrived, the cannon would be aimed only at the British earthworks, their dugout forts."

THE SHELLING CONTINUED ON into the night, but Pegg and Hannah continued their chores. Though every time a cannonball shot through the air, both girls looked up nervously.

That night, after they finished eating, Hannah lay in bed, tossing and turning. *How can I possibly stay with Pegg for weeks, maybe months?* she wondered. She twisted the ring Lizzie had given her as she thought about her friend. She also thought about her own father. *He had been stationed in Williamsburg, but where was he now? And where was David? Were they safe? Was Mother safe? And what of the siege of Yorktown? Would this war ever be over?* She said a prayer before falling into a restless sleep.

CHAPTER NINE
Going Home at Last

ON A CRISP, MID-OCTOBER MORNING, the cannon shots stopped as suddenly as they had started. The silence felt strange to Hannah, not surprising considering that cannon fire had been virtually continuous for the previous eight days. An hour later, a messenger rode a big brown horse into Williamsburg. "Cornwallis raised the white flag!" he shouted.

During the next couple of days different horsemen came into Williamsburg with varied news as the terms of surrender were debated. Early on the morning of the 19th, Hannah and Pegg rushed outside to hear a messenger cry "British surrender! Redcoats give up! Come to the surrender ceremony in the field near Mr. Moore's house at two o'clock." Hannah's heart leapt with joy. Washington had won a great victory. *Was this the end of the war?*

Hannah untied her red hair ribbon, and tossed it into the air. "It's over, Pegg! I can go home!" She turned to her sister. "You *will* come with me, won't you? Everyone will want to see General Cornwallis surrender."

"Now David will return," said Pegg, without answering Hannah's question.

"Yes! Yes!" said Hannah. "And Father, too!"

The street was crowded with civilians, all in good spirits. People swarmed out of their houses and into the street. Several men on horseback raced down the road toward Yorktown. A group of women, each carrying a bundle of food, loaded two horse-drawn wagons.

Carriages and wagons rattled along the narrow lane, filled with elated families. One boy leaned out of a cart. "Come to Yorktown!" he called to Hannah and Pegg. "See the Redcoats on their knees!"

"Let's go, Pegg!" Hannah urged. "We need to catch a ride before everyone else has left."

"I'm not going," said Pegg, shaking her head. "But I'll pack a lunch for you." She turned around and went back inside.

Hannah followed, staring at Pegg in disbelief. She watched as her sister reached into the barrel and pulled out two ripe apples. What was wrong? How could she even think of not going to Yorktown?

"Why, aren't you coming with me?" Hannah asked, dumbfounded.

"No, Hannah," said Pegg, opening the cupboard. She took out a strip of dried beef and a large piece of bread. She poured two cups of apple cider. "Here, Hannah," she said quietly, "sit down and drink this, and I'll tell you why I'm staying here." She drew in a breath, as if she had a lot on her mind.

"What's wrong?" Hannah asked, suddenly feeling a chill. It must be serious if Pegg didn't want to see their mother.

"It's nothing bad," Pegg murmured. "Actually, it's something wonderful." She smiled radiantly.

"Tell me!" demanded Hannah, unable to stand the suspense any longer.

"You see, Hannah," Pegg explained, taking a seat across from her sister. "I'm three months pregnant. I dare not travel over bumpy roads."

"You mean I'm going to be an aunt?" Hannah asked, a smile lighting her face.

"That's right," Pegg said, beaming. She rose and put Hannah's lunch into a sack. "I wrote to David about it, and he wrote back. He's very happy."

"I'm happy, too," said Hannah. "That's as exciting as Cornwallis's surrender!"

Pegg pulled an envelope from her apron pocket. "Give this to Mother," she said. "I wrote her a note about the good news. If it's a boy, I'll name him after Father."

"Joshua's a perfect name," Hannah said, taking the lunch bag. "I wish I could stay and celebrate the good news, but it's time for me to leave for Yorktown, Pegg." She paused. "I wish you would have told me about the baby earlier."

Pegg laughed. "What would you have done?" asked Pegg. "Stitch dainty little nightgowns?"

"Maybe I would have," said Hannah, grinning. "I definitely would have lifted heavy things for you."

"Nonsense," said Pegg. "I'm healthy as can be. There's nothing to worry about!" She kissed Hannah's forehead. "You look beautiful in my navy dress." Her eyes sparkled.

"Do you mind if I wear it home?" asked Hannah. "Or would you rather have me wear a plainer one?"

"I want you to have it, Hannah. In a couple of weeks, it won't even fit me."

"I love this dress," said Hannah. "Thank you, Pegg."

"You look much nicer now than you did when you first arrived," said Pegg. "I burned your muddy clothes as soon as I could." The girls laughed as Pegg walked

Hannah to the front door.

"Say hello to everyone for me," said Pegg.

Hannah hugged her sister. "I'll miss you," she said, softly.

"And I'll miss you, too, Hannah," Pegg answered. "I felt lonely until you arrived, but being with you has made my time away from David fly by." She hesitated. "You know, I've always envied the ease you feel with everybody—young and old. Everyone likes you, Hannah."

With tears in her eyes, Hannah opened the door. Leaving Pegg was more difficult than she would have thought. She'd never realized that Pegg actually envied *her*.

Minutes later, a wagon pulled by two horses turned onto the street. "I'll see if they'll take me," Hannah said. "It looks like there's room." She ran down the steps, turning back to blow Pegg a kiss.

"My prayers are with you," Pegg called, waving, but Hannah had already dashed down the street to hail the driver.

"ARE YOU HEADED FOR YORKTOWN?" the middle-aged driver called down to Hannah, pulling in his rein. He and his plump wife sat high on a wooden seat.

"Yes," Hannah answered. "May I have a ride?"

"Jump aboard," the woman said smiling.

"I'm Evans Conklin, and this is my wife, Sadie," the man said, flicking a whip across the horses' rumps. The wagon jolted forward.

"And who might you be?" Sadie Conklin asked.

"Hannah Winslow." Hannah settled herself in the back of the wagon, letting her legs dangle over the edge. "I'm pleased to meet you, Mr. and Mrs. Conklin."

She felt lucky to be riding with such friendly people. "Do you live in Williamsburg?" she asked, turning toward the driver's seat.

"We own a farm three miles from town," said Sadie. "What about you, lass?"

"I'm from Yorktown."

"It's been tough for the folks who live there. Have you heard that the British evacuated all the civilians?" said Evans, shaking his head. "I've heard that the past few weeks have been very difficult."

Hannah's heart felt a chill. *Was Mother safe? Martin? Lizzie?*

"And now the Redcoats are living in caves." Sadie chuckled.

"That's a change from the beginning of the war," said Hannah.

"Does your family still live in Yorktown?" asked Sadie.

"My mother," Hannah said. Then she turned back and watched the road. She wished the horses would go faster. "I'm worried my mother may not be there," she said quietly.

"Don't you worry, Hannah," Sadie said with confidence. "She'll be fine." Hannah felt a little better.

As they neared Yorktown, Hannah gazed at the open fields dotted with hundreds of tents. Groups of American soldiers laughed and talked and shined their boots. What pride they must feel to have defeated Cornwallis.

In contrast, Hannah was astonished to see that most of the British earthworks had been destroyed by cannonballs. Only a few had been left standing. The soil had been gouged and torn, and one farm on the outskirts had been ravaged. Hannah wondered what she'd find at home.

A little after noon, Mr. Conklin reined in the horses. "This is as far as we're going, Hannah," he said. "Sadie and I will be camping over there." He pointed to a meadow crowded with tents. People were milling about, waiting for the time and place of the surrender ceremony to be announced.

"Thank you for the ride," Hannah said, leaping off the wagon, onto the dusty road. "I just live up the road a short distance."

"I hope you find that all is well," Sadie said sympathetically.

"I'm sure my mother will be fine," Hannah replied. "Thank you again!"

After she passed through the two Allied siege lines and the abandoned British trenches, she hurried toward her house, her pulse racing. What would she find?

CHAPTER TEN

After the Battle

AS HANNAH RACED DOWN YORKTOWN'S Main Street, low thunder rumbled on the horizon. In the distance she glimpsed Secretary Nelson's mansion, which had been Cornwallis's headquarters. Evidently Cornwallis had evacuated it, for only the walls of the brick mansion remained. The blasted sides stood starkly against a gray sky and dark swirling clouds.

There wasn't a Redcoat in sight. The British tents had been moved back to the water's edge, their peaks dotted along the nearby fields. Their deserted camp looked somber and quiet.

As passing civilians picked through rubble that had once been their homes, Hannah felt overwhelmed with fear. Yorktown had changed so much. She remembered how safe she'd felt in Williamsburg.

She turned the corner and paused when she came to

Lizzie's house. The interior had been gutted by fire. A blackened roof and broken windows made it clear that the house was empty. Nothing stirred, except for a smoke-stained curtain, billowing out from an upstairs window.

Hannah held back her tears and continued on. When she saw her own white clapboard house intact, and her mother standing on the porch, relief took hold of her.

Hannah burst into tears as she rushed toward her mother's open arms. She hugged her mother, feeling warm and loved. "I missed you!" Hannah choked on the words.

"I missed you, too, Hannah," her mother said, holding her daughter close.

"It feels so good to be home," said Hannah, once she'd settled herself on the familiar sofa. Her mother sat beside her. "When the shelling started, I didn't know if I would ever see you again."

"So much has happened, Hannah," her mother said, with tear-filled eyes. Her mother pulled back, a smile and a tear on her face. "Half the town had to leave their homes and live in tents to escape the awful artillery. I lived in a tent below the bluff closer to the York River." Hannah could not picture her mother living in a tent.

"I don't know what I would have done without Martin. He helped me pitch my tent. Every night, the men would roast whatever meat they could find over a big bonfire." She paused, taking Hannah's hand. "To tell you the truth, I have never been so frightened in my life. Luckily, only the kitchen was damaged. The cannon fire made a terrible mess!"

"Have you heard from Father?" asked Hannah, hopefully.

"Not a word. But not an hour goes by that I don't pray for him."

"What happened to Lizzie's family?" Hannah asked, dreading the answer. What if Lizzie had been hurt—or killed?

"Their house caught fire when the shelling began," said Mrs. Winslow. "Lizzie and her mother left for Baltimore two weeks ago. They went to stay with Lizzie's aunt."

Hannah's heart sank. Would she ever see Lizzie again? She looked at her gold ring, knowing she'd never be able to replace such a dear and loyal friend. But at least Lizzie was safe.

Hannah got up and began to look around inside the house. When she looked outside at the kitchen, however, her jaw dropped. Four holes had been blown in the walls. Her mother had stuffed rags into each opening. The windowpanes had been shattered, with bits of glass covering the stove. Several chairs had been knocked over. Broken pots, crockery, and bricks from the fireplace littered the floor.

"It's such a jumble that I don't even know where to

start," said Mrs. Winslow. "Last night, when I moved back home, I plugged the holes in the walls. Martin has promised to mortar them and to mend the fireplace once the surrender ceremony is over." She attempted a smile. "We'll need to make do for now." For the first time, Hannah noticed wrinkles around her mother's eyes. Clearly, she was tired and discouraged.

"Never mind, Mother," said Hannah, knowing how upset her mother must feel. She picked up a chair. "I'll help put everything back just the way it was. A good cleaning will do wonders." Looking around at the debris she knew it would take more than a sweep of a broom.

"Sit down, Hannah," her mother said, wiping her face with a handkerchief. "I want to hear about your adventure. Martin told us you succeeded in delivering the maps to General Washington. Knowing British troops' positions enabled the Continental Army to close in faster; you did a brave and noble thing. I was also grateful to learn that you were staying with Pegg. Martin received word from one of the General's men." She smiled, and ran her hand over Hannah's cheek. "How good it is to have you home again!"

"I would have come sooner, but as soon as General Washington's men began their advance, no one was allowed to leave Williamsburg," said Hannah. "But Pegg and I had a wonderful visit."

"How is she?" Mrs. Winslow asked, her eyes lighting up at the mention of her elder daughter.

"Pegg is fine," Hannah said. "She's kept busy mending uniforms for soldiers." She fumbled in her pocket, and handed her mother the crumpled envelope. "This is for you."

Eagerly, Mrs. Winslow tore it open and read Pegg's letter, while Hannah waited impatiently for her to finish. When she did, her mother smiled with delight. "I'm going to be a grandmother! I wish your father were here to share the news. We'll bring Pegg home when her time comes."

It was nice to see her mother so happy and talkative. Hannah loved the idea of being an aunt.

"Now I know Pegg's news, but I haven't heard yours," said Mrs. Winslow. "Tell me what happened. I was so worried about you."

Hannah related the whole story to her mother, right down to her ride home with the Conklins.

"My little girl," Mrs. Winslow said proudly. "You were so courageous to pass through enemy lines." She squeezed her daughter's hand. "Martin brought us a fat chicken for dinner this afternoon after the British surrender. I'll go out back and clean it."

"I'll do some cleaning," Hannah said, rolling up her sleeves. She had learned a lot from Pegg about cleaning.

AN HOUR LATER, HANNAH STOOD and proudly surveyed the kitchen. She had cleaned and swept the floor, and scrubbed the stove.

Her mother came over, a plucked chicken in her hands, and nodded with approval. "You've done such a nice job, Hannah. I never thought I'd see my kitchen this neat again."

"More work needs to be done," said Hannah, "but at least we can use it now." Her mother agreed, smiling gratefully.

Though she was tired, her mother's praise filled Hannah with happiness.

CHAPTER ELEVEN
The Redcoats Surrender

WITH HER MOTHER'S APPROVAL, HANNAH walked toward the edge of town and out past the British trenches. As she neared the Allied lines, she began to hear the sound of music and marching. Climbing up onto the Grand Battery she saw a beautiful sight. Thousands of Continental soldiers in blue and tan uniforms formed a square, marching in time to the rat-a-tat of a drum. They were led by General Baron von Steuben. Although General von Steuben sounded gruff, he smiled as he puffed on his pipe. *Everybody will be smiling today*, Hannah thought, *except for the Redcoats.* She couldn't wait for the ceremony.

She watched a group of soldiers wearing fringed leather hunting shirts, moccasins, and round hats, sauntering by with tomahawks and long knives tucked into their belts. They were from the Pennsylvania backwoods.

Their loose formation displayed a dislike for rigid marching commands. Because they were excellent marksmen, however, they were forgiven a lack of discipline.

It was almost two o'clock in the afternoon; Hannah turned away from the parade and hurried home to dress quickly in her blue dress trimmed with green bows. The tight-fitting sash made her trim waist look even smaller. Tying back her thick auburn curls with a green ribbon, she looked in the mirror and smiled. She wanted to look her best on such an exciting day.

Mrs. Winslow entered the room, carrying a bucket of water. Hannah was afraid she would be reprimanded for wearing her good dress, but Mrs. Winslow didn't mention it. All she said was, "Come let us go and watch those proud British lay down their guns."

Hannah and her mother hurried outside of town to watch the festivities. She felt lucky to live so close to the action. She admired the banners and flags fluttering in the breeze. Flags also adorned houses and street lamps. A troop of cavalry, their plumes fluttering in the air, rode by.

"Mother," Hannah said enthusiastically, "look how handsome the Virginia Light Dragoons are." Her mother agreed. The soldiers, wearing black helmets with the horsehair crests, were quite a sight. The men looked straight ahead of them, holding their flags up high.

Hannah couldn't wait to see General Washington again. Would he be dressed as smartly as when she'd met him? Would he remember her?

Martin soon joined them on the way. "I'm proud of you, Hannah," he said, with a twinkle in his eye. "And I can't thank you enough."

"I can't thank *you* enough for helping my mother while I was gone," said Hannah.

HANNAH, HER MOTHER, AND MARTIN, along with many other people, reached the meadow Washington had chosen for the ceremony. No one wanted to miss Cornwallis's surrender.

"I wish Pegg were here to see this," Mrs. Winslow said, wistfully. A troop of soldiers marched past them.

"I tried to get her to come but—" Something caught Hannah's attention.

Sure enough, Mr. Winslow was one of the soldiers passing by. Seeing his wife and daughter, he flashed them a wide grin. Hannah saw her mother's eyes fill with tears of love and relief. Her father was safe, and looked younger and tanner than Hannah had remembered. Oh, what an amazing day!

"Look." Hannah pointed at two columns of soldiers

ahead of them. She guessed they were French and Continental. How proud and straight they stood. Even the tattered militiamen, with patches on their uniforms and toes poking out of their boots, held their heads high as they marched in formation, proud veterans and skilled marksmen that they were.

Soldiers and civilians alike waited in silence for the British troops to appear and march down the road between the French and American ranks.

General Washington appeared on a chestnut steed. He positioned himself at the head of his Continental troops, looking splendid in his blue uniform, polished boots, and tricornered hat. Although his expression was solemn, his eyes sparkled with joy.

Next, General Rochambeau, the French general, rode forth. Did he know that the Americans had nick-named him *Rush-on-boys?* In turn, General Rochambeau took his place at the head of the French column. The white and gold French uniforms glittered in the sun.

Suddenly, after an hour's wait, a drumbeat sounded, quieting the crowd. Standing at the base of a tree, a young American boy wearing a bearskin cap beat a drum. Hannah stood on her toes to see better. Next came the British drum and fife corps playing a mournful tune.

A troop of Redcoats marched forward, then halted.

Hannah was startled when an officer in a brilliant red coat and a tricornered hat burst forth from their ranks. Looking neither right nor left, he marched between the two enemy lines with his head held high, his posture perfectly straight. He walked toward Count de Rochambeau, but the French general, with a flick of his wrist, indicated he must approach General Washington.

"That isn't Cornwallis," a man growled in disappointment. "That's Brigadier General Charles O'Hara—an Irish officer!"

"Give us Cornwallis!" someone yelled.

Hannah looked everywhere for Cornwallis. Where was the British commander?

Muttered protests swept through the crowd. "Cornwallis is sick," one woman said, and then with a wink added, "Or so he says. I think he's pretending."

Another woman said, "He doesn't want to give up his sword to General Washington!"

General O'Hara, with an unwavering smile, turned and headed for General Washington. But the American general motioned O'Hara to present his sword to his second-in-command, General Benjamin Lincoln.

Again General O'Hara turned, this time to offer his sword to General Lincoln. While General Washington looked on, Lincoln soberly received the British sword of surrender.

The British had always regarded the Continental Army with scorn. The shame of surrendering to these colonists proved to be more than they could bear, and they refused to look into the eyes of their American victors.

The Redcoats marched to the meadow and laid down their muskets. Most soldiers stacked them neatly in piles, but a few hurled down their weapons angrily. Hannah noticed a few of them crying, while others wore angry scowls. Some British soldiers threw their guns with such vigor that the locks broke off. The grenadiers seemed to Hannah the most handsome soldiers, with tall helmets and knee-top boots. They carried grenades into battle. Clearly, they were unable to bear the disgrace of defeat.

General Washington rode down the path to the cheers of the onlookers. The Americans had won a mighty victory over King George III. Hannah and all of the colonists were more confident that England might soon sue for peace.

Oh, how tall and impressive General George Washington appears, Hannah thought. And she knew how warm he could be. She would never forget his kindness.

Suddenly, Hannah's heartbeat quickened. General

Washington had stopped his horse right in front of her. He leaned down and touched her shoulder. "It's patriots like you, Hannah Winslow, who have helped our cause."

Feeling her heart about to burst, Hannah managed a brilliant smile. "I was glad to help, sir," she replied.

From his jacket, the General unclasped a small green ribbon on a gold bar. "Please accept this as a token of my gratitude," he said, holding it out to her.

With trembling fingers, Hannah reached up to accept the ribbon. What an honor. Then with a salute, General George Washington rode on.

"Did I just see General George Washington saluting my own daughter?"

Hannah turned to find her father gazing down at her. "Father!" she cried, hugging him tight. Then he hugged his wife.

Then, while Mrs. Winslow pinned the green ribbon on Hannah's dress, Hannah told her father about her mission to Williamsburg. "I'm so proud of you, Hannah," he said, kissing his daughter's forehead. "Our little girl is a heroine!" he said to his wife.

Hannah was too overcome to speak. Suddenly, she burst into tears of happiness.

"It's time to go home," said her mother. "Will you be joining us for dinner?" she asked her husband.

Mr. Winslow nodded.

Yes, Hannah thought. *We'll all be together again.*

Hannah touched the ribbon General Washington had given her as she walked home with her mother and father.

THAT NIGHT HANNAH LAY IN her warm, cozy bed, listening to the rain. There were so many things to think about. For one thing, Yorktown would once again be a peaceful little town near the bay, without a Redcoat in sight. She wished Lizzie would return. Everything would be safe, and maybe Lizzie's house could be rebuilt.

Just as Yorktown seemed to be a turning point in the war, these past few weeks had been a turning point in Hannah's life. Somehow, she felt more grown-up. Her important mission to Williamsburg, and staying with Pegg, had taught her many things. Anticipating a bright future, Hannah drifted off to sleep.